All Aboard
CARS

Grosset & Dunlap

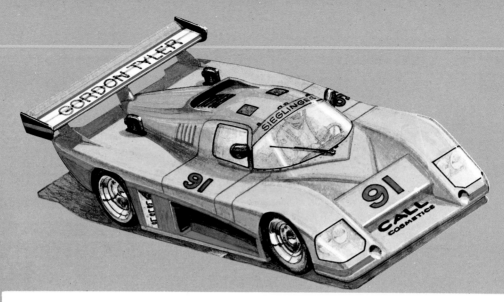

Library of Congress Cataloging-in-Publication Data

Weir, Catherine Daly.
  All aboard cars / by Catherine Daly Weir; illustrated by Courtney.
    p. cm.
  Summary: Text and illustrations introduce various types of automobiles including race cars, emergency vehicles, and cars of the future.
  1. Automobiles—Juvenile literature. [1. Automobiles.] 1. Courtney, ill.   II. Title.   III. Series.
  TL147.W45   1996
  629.222—dc20   95-22239
                                        2006 Printing   CIP
ISBN 0-448-41102-4   AC

Some of the illustrations in this book have appeared previously in *The Big Book of Real Race Cars and Race Car Driving*, published by Grosset & Dunlap, copyright © 1989 by Grosset & Dunlap, Inc.

Special thanks to Ford Motor Company and David Machaiek, Owls Head Transportation Museum, Owls Head, Maine.

All Aboard
CARS

By Catherine Daly Weir
Illustrated by Courtney

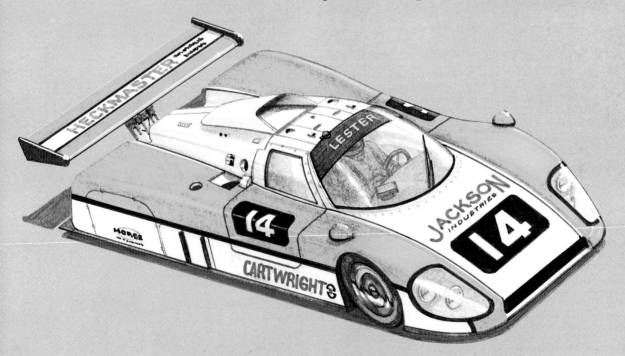

Grosset & Dunlap, Publishers

There are more than 400 million cars in the world today. They are everywhere—taking people to work, to school, and on vacations. But not so long ago, there were no cars at all. Most people used horses to get where they wanted to go.

The first "horseless carriages," like this Roper Steam Carriage, were powered by steam. They were noisy and dirty and had to stop often to wait for more steam to be made. The coal fires that heated the steam could be dangerous, too!

ROPER STEAM CARRIAGE, 1865

Other early cars, like the Mildé Electric, used electricity to run. Electric cars were clean and quiet, but they were slow and their heavy batteries needed recharging often.

MILDÉ ELECTRIC CAR, 1900

The first gasoline-powered cars were invented in the late 1800s. Gas cars were easy to drive and easier to refuel than steam or electric cars. But gas cars were also expensive. Only very rich people could afford them. Then in 1908, an American named Henry Ford built an inexpensive car that he called the Model T.

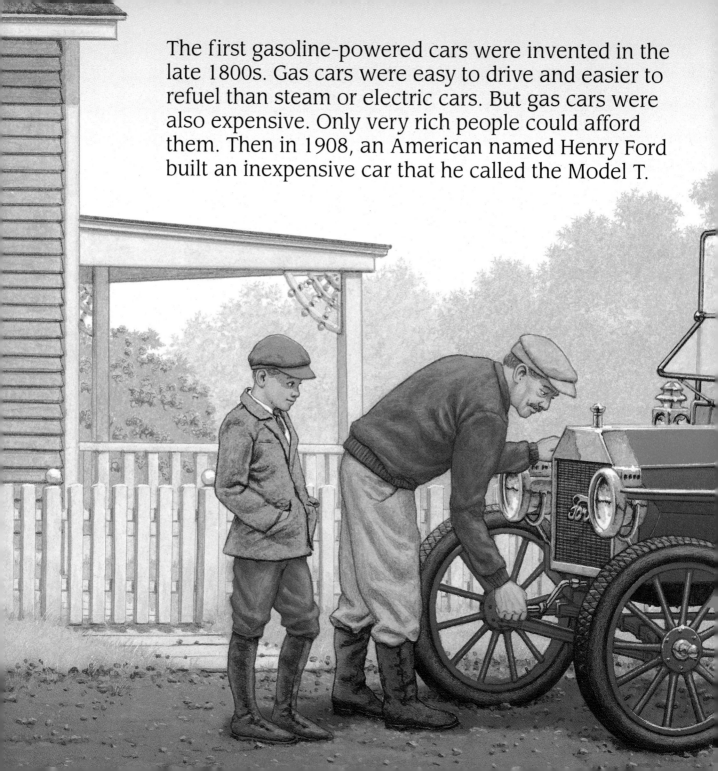

The first Model T was small and simple. It did not have bumpers or seat belts or a spare tire. To start the motor, you had to turn a crank, not a key like we do today. But it was a car almost everyone could afford.

FORD MODEL T, 1909

By the 1920s, millions of cars were on the roads. The Bugatti Royale was one of the largest and fanciest "luxury" cars. Like other luxury cars, it was big and comfortable and made for people who wanted to travel in style.

BUGATTI TYPE 41 ROYALE, 1927

MG TC, 1946

For drivers who were more interested in speed, "sports" cars were made. Their powerful engines and smaller, lighter bodies allowed them to go much faster than regular cars.

   This two-seater MG TC could go as fast as 125 miles per hour. The convertible top and even the front windshield could fold down for open-air driving.

Today, some cars are built just to do special jobs. Most police cars start out as ordinary cars. Then lights and sirens are added. They are used to warn other cars to get out of the way or to tell them to pull over. A screen called a "cage" between the front and back seats holds suspects.

The fire chief has a special car, too. It has lights and a siren so the chief can get to emergencies quickly.

FIRE CHIEF'S CAR

POLICE CAR

A taxicab takes people to places for a fee. Most taxis have a meter that keeps track of how far the cab goes and shows the passenger how much to pay.

TAXICAB

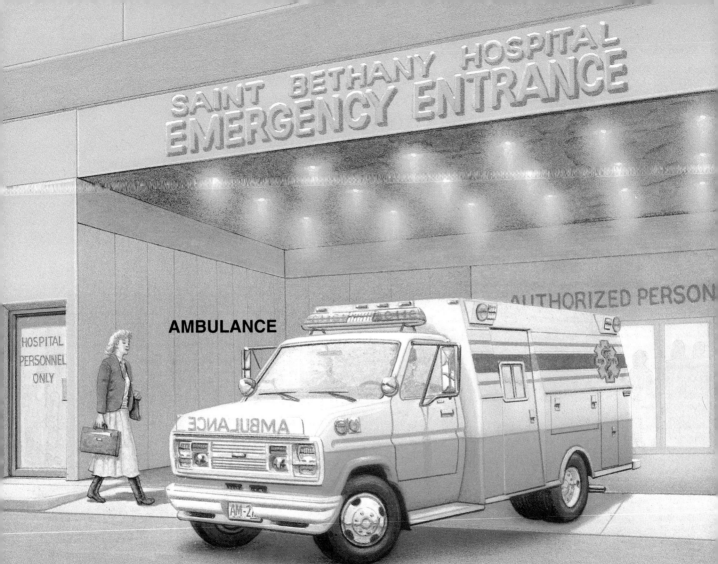

WEE-AHH! WEE-AHH! There goes an ambulance. When someone is sick or hurt and needs to get to the hospital fast, an ambulance is called. Ambulances have stretchers, blankets, and other emergency equipment. Some even have teddy bears for young passengers to hold.

U.S. ARMY JEEP, 1941

Jeeps first were used during World War II to help soldiers carry supplies and move from place to place. They can go over rough, bumpy ground that would stop other cars in their tracks. This all-purpose vehicle can even be used as an ambulance in an emergency.

WORLD'S LONGEST LIMOUSINE

Some cars are built just for fun. This custom-built limousine is the longest car in the world. It is 104 feet long—almost as long as three city buses. It even has a putting green!

Some cars are built just to go fast. Race cars are made to be driven by specially trained drivers on specially built tracks. Automobile racing is one of the toughest and most dangerous sports in the world. To protect themselves, drivers wear cushioned helmets, face masks, and fire-resistant clothing—down to their underwear!

There are different kinds of race cars for different kinds of car races. Formula One cars are one type of race car. They ride very low to the ground and have the engine in the rear.

FORMULA ONE CAR

MONACO GRAND PRIX

One of the most glamorous car races of all is the
Monaco Grand Prix (grahn PREE). Every spring,
Formula One cars drive through the streets of Monte
Carlo, the capital of Monaco, at speeds up to 200 miles
per hour.

Indy cars look a lot like Formula One racers. But Indy cars are even faster and sturdier. They have to be—Indy races are very long.

The most famous Indy race is the Indianapolis 500, a 500 mile race held on Memorial Day each year. It is one of the fastest car races in the world—and one of the longest. Drivers race around the two-and-a-half-mile track 200 times—in three and a half hours!

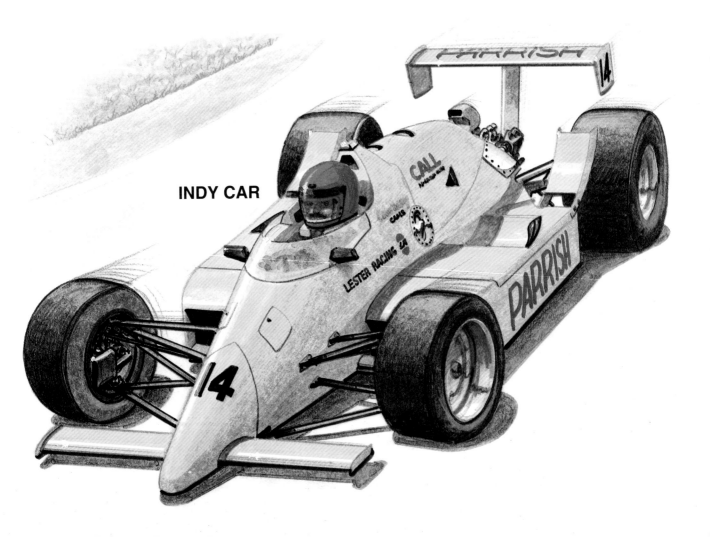

INDY CAR

TOP FUEL CAR

Top Fuel Cars, or "Dragsters," race on straight tracks called "strips" that are one-quarter of a mile long. They can reach speeds of more than 260 miles per hour in less than six seconds. Dragsters go so fast they need parachutes to help them stop.

BUDWEISER ROCKET

The fastest car in the world is the three-wheeled Budweiser Rocket. It is thirty-nine feet long and less than two feet wide. Powered by a jet engine, the Budweiser Rocket can go 739 miles per hour—faster than most airplanes can fly!

A stock car may look like a regular car, but it sure doesn't drive like one! The engine is taken out and completely rebuilt—or "souped up"—so the car can go more than 200 miles per hour. Because stock cars can reach such dangerously high speeds, a steel frame called a "roll cage" is welded inside. It keeps the roof from collapsing if the car flips over.

STOCK CAR

PIT STOP

The Daytona 500 is a famous stock car race held each year at the Daytona International Speedway in Florida. In long races like the Daytona 500, drivers must pull over for several pit stops. Each car has its own pit and pit crew. The crew cleans the windshield, fills the tank with gas, changes the tires, and makes any needed repairs.

In a car race, every second counts, so pit crews work fast. A smooth pit stop can take as little as fifteen seconds.

SELF-SERVICE GAS STATION

GAS PUMP

A visit to the service station is a lot like a pit stop, only it doesn't have to happen at lightning speed.

GARAGE

Some gas stations are full-service. The attendant may clean the windshield, check the oil, and fill the gas tank. Other stations are self-service. The customer pumps her own gas. She may want to fill her tires with air, too.

If an oil change, a repair, or a tune-up is needed, the car goes into the garage. It is jacked up on a lift so the mechanic can get a better look.

Car companies are always trying to build better cars—cars that use less gasoline, cars that are safer, and cars that are better for the environment.

Some cars of the future might be solar-powered or run on rechargeable batteries. They might even be able to drive both on land and under water. Who knows what kind of car *you* may be driving someday!

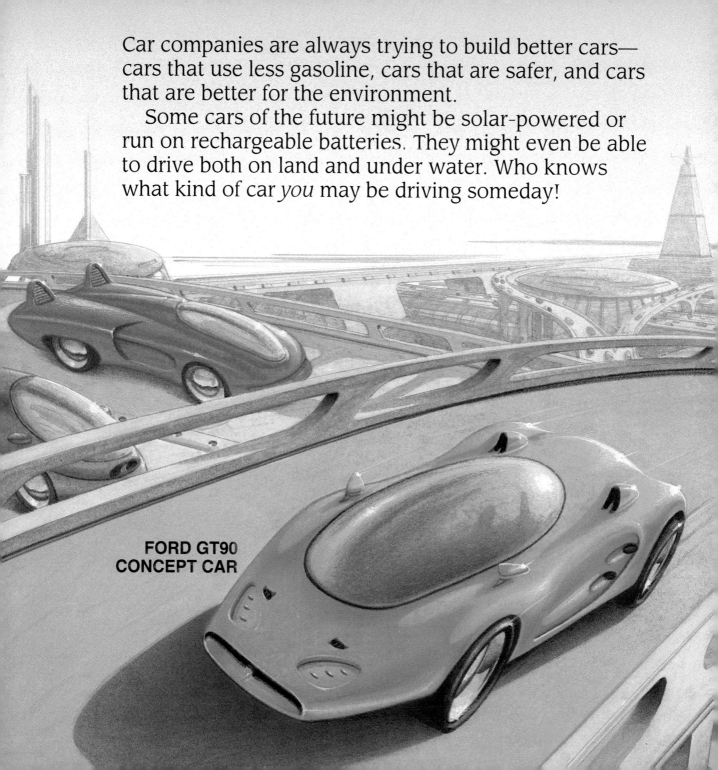

FORD GT90
CONCEPT CAR